Texting with...

Black History

Martin Luther King, Jr.
-
Sojourner Truth
-
Aretha Franklin

Written by Bobby Basil

3 FREE BOOKS!

Go to bobbybasilwriter.com!

Hi! I'm Alex!

I'm nine, and I don't know
what I want to be
when I grow up.

There are so many
amazing things to do!

My mom helps me text with
important people and ask them
questions about their lives.

It's fun to ask questions!

Today
my mom and I are
texting with...

Dr. Martin Luther King, Jr.!

Dr. King was a minister
and activist during the
Civil Rights Movement
that lived from 1929 until 1968.

He advanced civil rights
through nonviolence
and civil disobediance.

I can't wait to text him
my questions!

Hi,
Dr. King!

Hi Alex!

Thank you
for texting
with me.

You're
welcome.

What do you
look like?

I look like
this...

Where were
you born?

I was born in
Atlanta,
Georgia.

What was your childhood like?

I sang in my church's choir as a boy.

I love singing!

It was difficult growing up in Atlanta, though.

Why is that?

Atlanta had laws separating black people from white people. It was called segregation. I felt the terrible effects of it every day.

That's an awful law!

It was. When I was a child, I had a white friend, but his father said we couldn't play together.

Because he was white and you were black?

Yes. The feeling of prejudice went beyond the law. Many people believed in their hearts that black people were bad.

But that's wrong!

It is. It made me angry growing up and watching people treat my family poorly because of the color of our skin.

I'm getting angry just thinking about it!

You should feel angry. Many times I watched my father stand up for himself when someone treated him poorly.

That was very brave of your dad to do, especially because of those bad laws!

My father was brave. I followed in his footsteps. I decided to become a minister so I could speak out against these problems.

That's good!

In 1955, another person challenged the wrongful law. Her name was Rosa Parks.

How did she challenge the law?

She was sitting on a bus, and she refused to give her seat to a white person. This broke the law, and she was arrested.

But she was sitting there first! That's not fair!

This law was never fair. I organized a bus boycott and told black people not to ride the bus because of the bad law. The bus company got very angry because they were losing money, and many people got very angry at me.

But you were standing up for yourself!

I was changing the way things always had been, and that is hard for many people to take.

Did the boycott work?

Yes. We boycotted the bus for 385 days, and the court changed the law making it illegal to segregate buses.

Wow! It must have been hard to boycott for that long. 385 days is more than a year!

Yes, it was hard for many people. Some chose to walk over 20 miles to work instead of riding the bus.

That's a long way to walk!

Standing against injustice is difficult, but you can't give up. The more people work together, the stronger you become.

Did the bus boycott end segregation everywhere?

Sadly, it did not. There still was much work to do.

That's how I feel when I clean my room. I clean it one day, and then before I know it my room is dirty again!

The world is like your room, Alex. We always need to make it better, and there is always more to do.

What did you do next?

I went to Birmingham, Alabama and used nonviolent tactics to bring attention to the ugliness of segregation. I led protests, marches, and had people sit in segregated areas to challenge the law.

If you break a law that's wrong, then I think that's the right thing to do.

I agree. That's called civil disobedience.

Did your civil disobedience work?

It did. TV stations broadcast the evil ways the government and police were treating us. The world took notice.

Did that end segregation?

No, but our protests helped move our cause forward.

Oh, come on, Dr. King! After all your hard work, segregation still existed?!

The arc of the moral universe is long, but it bends toward justice. Remember your bedroom, Alex.

There's always more work to be done...

Exactly.

But I'm getting so upset that all your hard work didn't solve the problem.

It takes a long time to change the world.

I guess you're right. I just wish the world changed faster. So what did you do next?

I helped lead a march on Washington, D.C.

Over 200,000 people joined me. It was there in America's capital where I gave a speech.

What was the speech about?

I said how I had a dream that one day we all could get along no matter the color of our skin.

I like that dream a lot!

Many other people did, too.

After I gave that speech, we started to see more progress. The next year, the government passed the Civil Rights Act, which outlawed discrimination based on race for voting, schools, and jobs.

I'm so happy for you, Dr. King!

Thank you. But passing that law did not end the struggle.

There still was a struggle, even after all that?

The struggle continues to this day.

I feel sad about all the struggles people have in their lives.

I do, too. I spoke out against other struggles in America, not just about race. I spoke about how poor people should get more help and how we should not fight in wars.

And I bet those struggles still exist, too.

They do, Alex. But people are working all over the world to make sure things are improving. We all need to try to help one another.

I have one more question for you.

Okay!

Do you think I should be a social activist when I grow up?

You have a big heart but get discouraged when thinking about all the world's problems. You need to know that you can make a difference, even if it will take time.

Thank you for the advice!

You're welcome!

It was fun talking to
Dr. King!

I think I want to be a
social activist now.

But there are a lot more
social activists
I can text
to learn more.

I can't wait to text
the next one!

FUN QUESTIONS FOR YOU FROM . . .
MARTIN LUTHER KING, JR.
WRITE YOUR ANSWERS IN THE TEXTING BUBBLES!

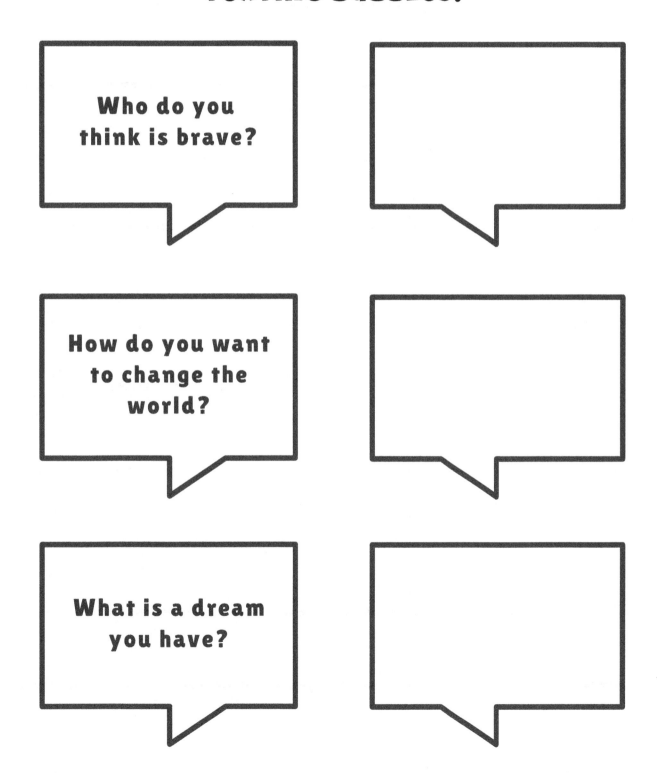

Who do you think is brave?

How do you want to change the world?

What is a dream you have?

COMPARE AND CONTRAST WITH . . .
MARTIN LUTHER KING, JR.

How are you and Dr. King the same?

_____

_____

_____

_____

How are you and Dr. King different?

_____

_____

_____

_____

THINKING ABOUT THE LIFE OF . . .
MARTIN LUTHER KING, JR.

How did Dr. King's life make you feel?

_____

_____

_____

_____

Would you want to live a day in Dr. King's life? Why or why not?

_____

_____

_____

_____

LEARNING FROM . . .
MARTIN LUTHER KING, JR.

What did you find most interesting about Dr. King's life?

_____

_____

_____

_____

What did Dr. King teach you?

_____

_____

_____

_____

WHAT FIVE W QUESTIONS WOULD YOU TEXT MARTIN LUTHER KING, JR.?

1. Who _____ ?

2. What _____ ?

3. When _____ ?

4. Where _____ ?

5. Why _____ ?

Meme Time With . . .
MARTIN LUTHER KING, JR.

DRAW A PICTURE THAT DESCRIBES
MARTIN LUTHER KING, JR.'S LIFE!

"The time is always right to do what is right."

- Martin Luther King, Jr.

"Injustice anywhere is a threat to justice everywhere."
- Martin Luther King, Jr.

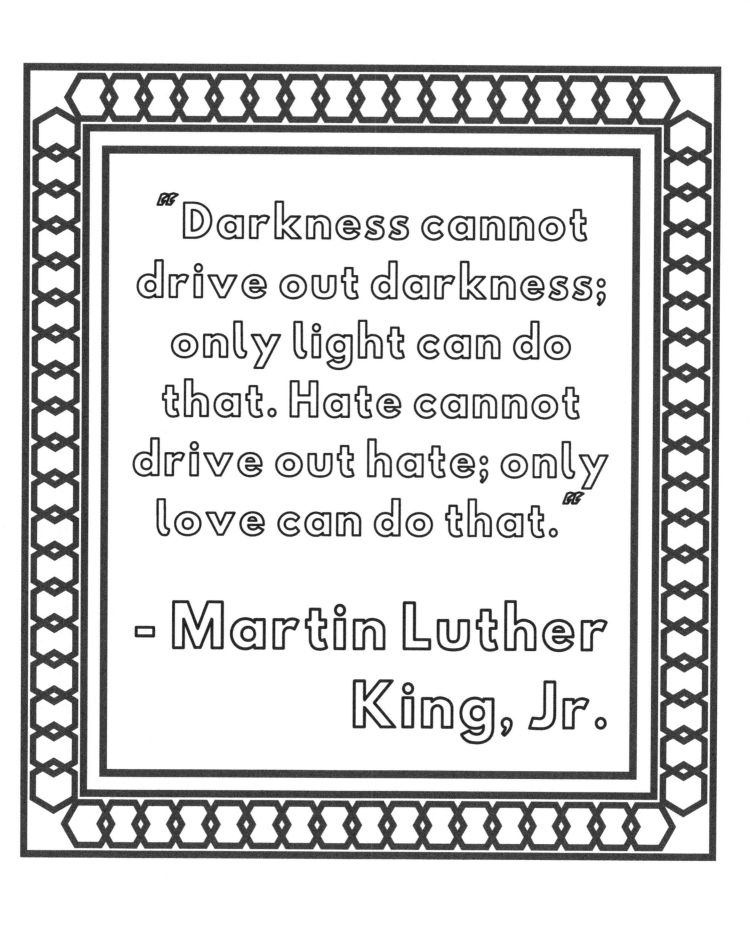

Texting with...

Sojourner Truth

A Social Activism Book

Written by Bobby Basil

Hi! I'm Alex!

I'm nine, and I don't know
what I want to be
when I grow up.

There are so many
amazing things to do!

My mom helps me text with
important people and ask them
questions about their lives.

It's fun to ask questions!

Today
my mom and I are
texting with...

Sojourner Truth!

Sojourner Truth was
an American abolitionist
and women's rights activist
that lived from 1797 until 1883.

She traveled across America
speaking about equality.

I can't wait to text her
my questions!

Hi Sojourner!

Hi Alex!

Thank you for texting with me.

You're welcome.

What do you look like?

I look like this...

Where were you born?

I was born in Swartekill, New York.

What was your childhood like?

I was born into slavery.

What's slavery?

Slavery is where people sell other people like they are pieces of property.

That's terrible!

Yes, it is terrible. And it happened for hundreds of years in America.

When I was nine years old, I was sold with a flock of sheep for $100. My new owner was cruel and harsh to me.

I'm sorry all of this happened to you.

Why did people think slavery was okay?

Many people in my time believed that black people were not human beings.

But every person on earth is a human being!

When America wrote the first laws called The Constitution, they said a black person was only 3/5 of a person.

That's the worst law ever!

I was sold to a new owner when I was 11, then again when I was 13.

I'm nine now, and I don't like thinking about someone selling me to another person like property.

Children were sold as slaves all the time in America. When I was 29, I escaped to freedom with my baby.

I'm glad you escaped!

I had to leave my other children in order to escape successfully.

That must have been a tough choice to make.

Luckily, New York passed a law in 1827 that ended slavery in the state.

That's great!

When I returned for my children, I learned my former owner illegally sold my son Peter to an owner in Alabama.

He sold your son?!

Yes, but the law was on my side. I went to court and won the case!

Yay!!! Was that hard to do?

Yes. I was one of the first black women to go to court against a white man and win.

People should treat everyone with kindness!

Yes. I traveled across America to tell people that.

I spoke about how America needed to abolish slavery. I also spoke about the need for women's rights.

What are women's rights?

Many people didn't think that women deserved equal rights as men, so I fought for these rights.

I'm angry that you had so many mean people in your life.

The world is full of injustice. We all can help stop the injustice and make the world better.

I gave a speech that said women and black people should have the same rights as everyone else.

Of course they should!

I'm glad you feel that way. No one is born with hate. It needs to be taught.

My mom doesn't teach me about hate. Even when I say I hate broccoli, she tells me that I should just say I don't like broccoli.

Your mom sounds like a wonderful person.

She is!

When you gave speeches, did people change their mind?

Maybe some did. All across America, people were changing their minds about slavery. America fought itself in the Civil War over if slavery should be legal.

I think I heard about that war! That's the one with Abraham Lincoln, right?

Yes, Abraham Lincoln was the president during the Civil War.

I think I want to text with him.

You should. I met him while I was helping America win the war and end slavery.

I feel like I can't make as big of a difference as you did.

Everyone can make a difference. Every choice we make is like a ripple that affects the world, both good and bad.

So I should make choices that help the world?

Yes, and if you really believe in something, tell others about it. Talk to your friends or even give speeches if you want.

I like giving speeches. Probably my favorite day in school is Show and Tell Day.

Show people a problem and tell them how to fix it.

There's a group of kids at school who say girls aren't smart. But that's wrong!

You're right. Girls are very smart.

Maybe I could talk to them?

That's a great idea, Alex.

I'll talk to them tomorrow!

Sometimes it takes people a long time to change their mind, but that shouldn't stop you from trying.

I have one more question for you.

Okay!

Do you think I should be a social activist when I grow up?

You want to make the world a better place, and that is what a social activist does.

But you can be a
social activist
with your actions
while still having
another job!

Thank you
for the
advice!

You're
welcome!

It was fun talking to
Sojourner Truth!

I think I want to be a
social activist now.

But there are a lot more
social activists
I can text
to learn more.

I can't wait to text
the next one!

FUN QUESTIONS FOR YOU FROM . . .
SOJOURNER TRUTH
WRITE YOUR ANSWERS IN THE TEXTING BUBBLES!

How do you want to make a difference?

Is there something you think is unjust?

What topic do you want to give a speech about?

COMPARE AND CONTRAST WITH . . .
SOJOURNER TRUTH

How are you and Sojourner the same?

_____

_____

_____

_____

How are you and Sojourner different?

_____

_____

_____

_____

THINKING ABOUT THE LIFE OF . . .
SOJOURNER TRUTH

How did Sojourner's life make you feel?

_____

_____

_____

_____

Would you want to live a day in Sojourner's life? Why or why not?

_____

_____

_____

_____

LEARNING FROM . . .
SOJOURNER TRUTH

What did you find most interesting about Sojourner's life?

_____

_____

_____

_____

What did Sojourner teach you?

_____

_____

_____

_____

WHAT FIVE W QUESTIONS WOULD YOU TEXT SOJOURNER TRUTH?

1. Who _____ ?

2. What _____ ?

3. When _____ ?

4. Where _____ ?

5. Why _____ ?

Meme Time With . . .
SOJOURNER TRUTH

DRAW A PICTURE THAT DESCRIBES SOJOURNER TRUTH'S LIFE!

"Truth is powerful and it prevails."

- Sojourner Truth

"It is the mind that makes the body."

- Sojourner Truth

"If women want rights more than they got, why don't they just take them, and not be talking about it."

- Sojourner Truth

Texting with...

Aretha Franklin

A Black History Biography Book for Kids

Written by Bobby Basil

Hi! I'm Alex!

I'm nine, and I don't know
what I want to be
when I grow up.

There are so many
amazing things to do!

My mom helps me text with
important people and ask them
questions about their lives.

It's fun to ask questions!

Today
my mom and I are
texting with...

Aretha Franklin!

Aretha Franklin was an
American singer,
songwriter, and pianist
that lived from 1942 until 2018.

Her nickname was
"The Queen of Soul."

I can't wait to text her
my questions!

Hi Aretha!

Hi Alex!

Thank you
for texting
with me.

You're
welcome.

What do you
look like?

I look like this...

Where were you born?

I was born in Memphis, Tennessee.

Is that where you grew up?

My dad moved our family to Detroit, Michigan when I was five.

Why did your dad move your family?

He got a job being a pastor at New Bethel Baptist Church in Detroit. He was nicknamed "The Million Dollar Voice."

Why was that his nickname?

He gave very emotional sermons. People paid him a lot of money to give sermons across America.

What did your mother do?

My mother died when I was nine.

I'm sorry.

I had several strong women that helped raise me, including my grandmother and the famous gospel singer Mahalia Jackson. After my mother passed away, I started to sing solos at my dad's church.

That sounds fun!

It was! My dad started to take me around the country to sing when he preached.

I like traveling. You get to see a lot of new things.

You're right. I also got to meet a lot of interesting people, like the singer Sam Cooke and Dr. Martin Luther King, Jr.

Did you get to sing a lot?

I did. When I was eighteen, I signed a record contract with Colombia Records.

What are records?

They were how people listened to music before the internet.

A record is a circle and rotates on a turntable.

I think my uncle with the funny beard has a record player!

They are becoming popular again. Whenever I sang, I sang with emotion. People started calling me "The Queen of Soul."

You were emotional like your dad with the million dollar voice!

Exactly! In 1966, I moved to Atlantic Records.

Were you glad you moved?

I was. At Atlantic, I released many of my most famous songs. I blended Gospel, Soul, R&B, and Pop.

I'm in the school choir!

Do you like singing?

I do. It makes me feel free when I sing.

That's how I felt, too. In 1967, I released the song "Respect" and that became my signature song.

What's a signature song?

It's a song that people associate with a singer. That song was about a strong woman who demanded respect, like me.

Everyone should have respect.

Yes. But in the 1960s in America, not everyone was getting respect.

Why not?

Black Americans were not allowed to drink at the same water fountains as white Americans.

That doesn't make sense!

Some people believed black people were not equal to white people. The Civil Rights movement protested this inequality.

Everyone should be treated the same! I would have protested with you!

My song "Respect" became a song that represented the Civil Rights Movement because we were demanding respect.

Did you get respect?

We gained many rights because of the movement. But there still is a lot of inequality in America today. And many people died fighting for justice.

My friend Martin Luther King, Jr. was killed fighting for equality. I sang at his funeral in 1968.

That's sad.

It is. But you have to fight for what is right. Sometimes singing from your heart helps to heal.

Did you keep making music?

Yes. In my life, I released 42 studio albums, 6 live albums, 45 compilation albums, and 131 singles.

That's a lot of music!

I was the first woman chosen for the Rock and Roll Hall of Fame. I won 18 Grammy music awards and sold more than 75 million records.

So many people got to hear you sing!

And people can still hear me sing, which is nice to think.

I have one more question for you.

Okay!

Do you think I should be a singer when I grow up?

If you feel the most joy when you sing and it makes you feel part of something bigger than yourself, then you should be a singer.

Thank you for the advice!

You're welcome!

It was fun talking to
Aretha Franklin!

I think I might want to be
a singer now.

But there are a lot more singers
I can text to learn more.

I can't wait to text
the next one!

FUN QUESTIONS FOR YOU FROM . . .
ARETHA FRANKLIN
WRITE YOUR ANSWERS IN THE TEXTING BUBBLES!

What do you love to do?

Who do you respect in your life?

What injustice do you want to make better?

COMPARE AND CONTRAST WITH . . .
ARETHA FRANKLIN

How are you and Aretha the same?

_____

_____

_____

_____

How are you and Aretha different?

_____

_____

_____

_____

THINKING ABOUT THE LIFE OF . . .
ARETHA FRANKLIN

How did Aretha's life make you feel?

_____

_____

_____

_____

Would you want to live a day in Aretha's life?
Why or why not?

_____

_____

_____

_____

LEARNING FROM . . .
ARETHA FRANKLIN

What did you find most interesting about Aretha's life?

_____

_____

_____

_____

What did Aretha teach you?

_____

_____

_____

_____

WHAT FIVE W QUESTIONS WOULD YOU TEXT ARETHA FRANKLIN?

1. Who _____ ?

2. What _____ ?

3. When _____ ?

4. Where _____ ?

5. Why _____ ?

MEME TIME WITH ...
ARETHA FRANKLIN

DRAW A PICTURE THAT DESCRIBES ARETHA FRANKLIN'S LIFE!

"Every
birthday is a
gift. Every
day is a gift."

- Aretha
Franklin

"Sometimes, what you're looking for is already there."

- Aretha Franklin

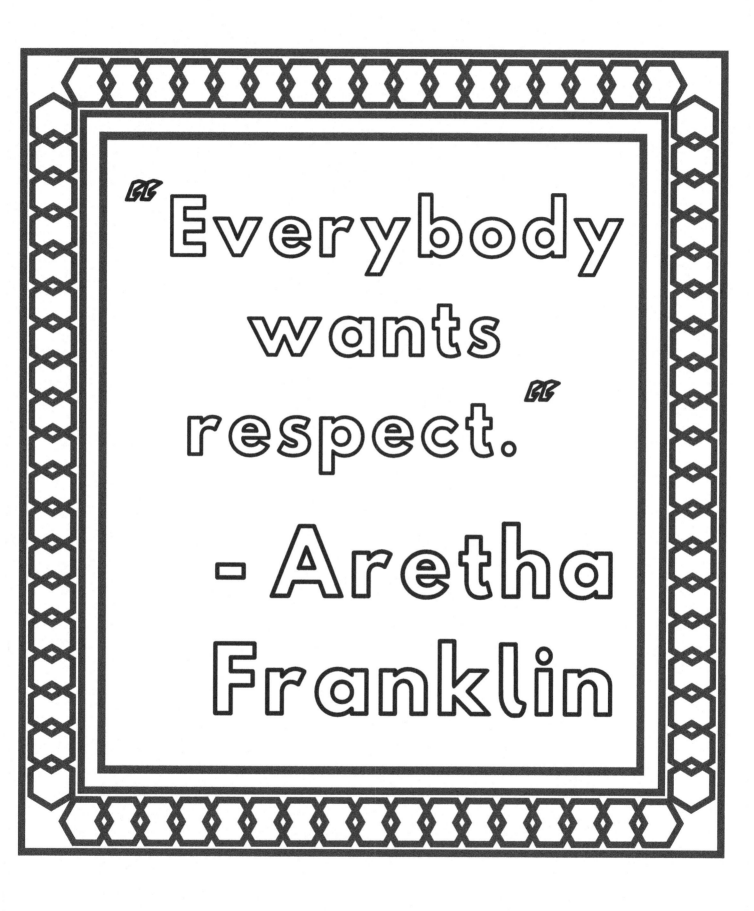

PLEASE LEAVE A REVIEW ON AMAZON!

Your review will help other readers discover my books. Thank you!

Made in the USA
Coppell, TX
07 February 2020

15507084R00063